Dear Parents:

Congratulations! Your child is taking the first steps on an exciting journey. The destination? Independent reading!

STEP INTO READING® will help your child get there. The progra~~m~~ five steps to reading success. Each step includes fun stories and co~~lorful~~ art or photographs. In addition to original fiction and books with f~~amiliar~~ characters, there are Step into Reading Non-Fiction Readers, Phonics Readers and Boxed Sets, Sticker Readers, and Comic Readers—a complete literacy program with something to interest every child.

Learning to Read, Step by Step!

Ready to Read   Preschool–Kindergarten
• big type and easy words • rhyme and rhythm • picture clues
For children who know the alphabet and are eager to begin reading.

Reading with Help   Preschool–Grade 1
• basic vocabulary • short sentences • simple stories
For children who recognize familiar words and sound out new words with help.

Reading on Your Own   Grades 1–3
• engaging characters • easy-to-follow plots • popular topics
For children who are ready to read on their own.

Reading Paragraphs   Grades 2–3
• challenging vocabulary • short paragraphs • exciting stories
For newly independent readers who read simple sentences with confidence.

Ready for Chapters   Grades 2–4
• chapters • longer paragraphs • full-color art
For children who want to take the plunge into chapter books but still like colorful pictures.

STEP INTO READING® is designed to give every child a successful reading experience. The grade levels are only guides; children will progress through the steps at their own speed, developing confidence in their reading.

Remember, a lifetime love of reading starts with a single step!

Published in the United States by Random House Children's Books, a division of
Penguin Random House LLC, 1745 Broadway, New York, NY 10019, and in Canada by
Penguin Random House Canada Limited, Toronto. The works in this collection were
originally published separately in slightly different form by Scholastic Inc. as *Scooby-Doo
and the Haunted Diner* in 2010; *Howling on the Playground* in 2000; *The Movie Star
Mystery* in 2009; *The Race Car Monster* in 2001; and *Snack Snatcher* in 2001.

Step into Reading, Random House, and the Random House colophon are registered
trademarks of Penguin Random House LLC.

Visit us on the Web!
StepIntoReading.com
rhcbooks.com

Educators and librarians, for a variety of teaching tools, visit us at
RHTeachersLibrarians.com

ISBN 978-0-593-43121-4 (trade)

MANUFACTURED IN CHINA

10 9 8 7 6 5 4 3 2

SCOOBY-DOO!
SNACKS AND SCARES!

A Collection of Five
Step 2 Early Readers

Random House 🏠 New York

CONTENTS

The Haunted Diner

by Mariah Balaban
illustrated by Duendes del Sur

Random House 🏠 New York

Scooby-Doo and the gang are on a road trip.

It starts to rain.

They stop at a diner.

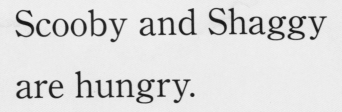

Scooby and Shaggy
are hungry.

They order a lot of food!
Outside, the storm gets worse.

The lights go out!
Shaggy and Scooby
are scared.

They hear a spooky moan.

It sounds like a monster!

Shaggy and Scooby jump up.

Shaggy and Scooby run to the kitchen to hide from the monster.

Zoinks!

Scooby and Shaggy run
out of the kitchen.

The lights come back on.
The ghost is gone!

Scooby and Shaggy's friends are gone, too. Scooby and Shaggy think the ghost got their friends!

Scooby and Shaggy
rush out of the diner.

They want to hide.
Shaggy finds the
door to the cellar.

Scooby and Shaggy hide.
They hear a howl.
Someone is saying
their names!

The cellar door opens.

Creak!

A shadow falls over
Scooby and Shaggy.

Fred, Daphne, and Velma

appear behind the witch.

The witch takes off
her hood.
It is the waitress
from the diner!
She is wearing
a rain poncho.

The gang leaves
the cellar.
Shaggy and Scooby
tell them that the
diner is haunted!

The waitress tells them
that the spooky moan
was from the jukebox.

Scooby and Shaggy tell them about the ghost in the kitchen.

There is no ghost.

That was the cook.

He was just covered

in flour!

Velma, Daphne, and Fred were outside getting flashlights.

The diner is not
haunted after all!
One last mystery—
when is lunch?

Soon, the waitress brings out a huge tray of food. The mystery is solved!

STEP INTO READING®

STEP 2

READING WITH HELP

HOWLING ON THE PLAYGROUND

by Gail Herman

illustrated by Duendes del Sur

Random House 🏠 New York

Scooby and the gang
are helping to build
a playground!

A woman walks over.

She is not happy.

The woman is named Edna.
Edna does not want a
playground by her house.
She says they are loud!

Drew, the person in charge, tells the gang to keep building.

The next day, the gang works on the sandbox.

"Sandbox" sounds a lot like "lunch box." Scooby and Shaggy get hungry!

Edna is back.
She says she heard
werewolves howling
the night before.

She says this is no place
for a playground
The gang hears her.
It sounds like there is
a mystery to solve!

That night, the gang
stays at the playground.
Scooby and Shaggy
are scared.

They do not like
werewolves!
They want to leave.
Velma stops them.

Daphne gives Scooby
a Scooby Snack.

Scooby and Shaggy
will help now.

Oww-ooo!

Scooby and Shaggy
hear a howl.
It is the werewolves!

Scooby and Shaggy

run away.

Shaggy bumps into
the swing set.
Ouch!

Oww-ooo!

The werewolves
keep howling.
Scooby and Shaggy
try to run up the slide
to hide.

They fall down.

Daphne, Velma, and Fred
find them.

Scooby and Shaggy hide

by some sandbags.

They hear another howl.

Scooby and Shaggy find
puppies sitting
on the sandbags!

Velma, Fred, and Daphne
see the puppies, too.
The puppies are howling
because they are hungry.

There are no werewolves!
Edna and Drew join them.

The gang shows them
the puppies.

Edna decides to take
the puppies home.

Edna likes the
playground now.

It is a great place
for the puppies to play!

It is another

mystery solved

by Mystery Inc.!

THE MOVIE STAR MYSTERY

by Karl Sturk

illustrated by Duendes del Sur

Random House 🏠 New York

The gang is at the Golden Knight Awards. There are a lot of movie stars!

Chase Saint John
always wins.
Lyle Glitz always loses.

Something is wrong. The police talk to Glenda, the host.

Fred, Velma, and Daphne race off to look for clues.

Scooby and Shaggy

are distracted by the food.

Scooby and Shaggy
look for a light switch.

Creak!

They hear footsteps
behind them.

Scooby and Shaggy find a dressing room.

A masked man appears.
Uh-oh!

He tries to grab
Shaggy and Scooby.

Scooby and Shaggy
run away.
The masked man
chases them.

VAULT

Scooby and Shaggy
find an empty vault.
They jump inside to hide.

Clang!

The masked man traps them in the vault.

Scooby and Shaggy
are very scared.

It is Daphne, Fred, and Velma! Glenda and a police officer are with them.

Fred catches
the masked man.

Fred removes the mask.

It is Lyle Glitz!

Lyle is mad that he never wins an award. He stole the envelopes so that no one could win this year.

Lyle returns the envelopes.

The gang rushes back
to the awards.

THE RACE CAR MONSTER

by Gail Herman

illustrated by Duendes del Sur

Random House 🏠 New York

Scooby and the gang
are at a racetrack.
They have free tickets
to a car race!

Shaggy and Scooby
want food.
They leave their friends.

Shaggy and Scooby
see a monster!
They run and hide
in the Mystery Machine.

Scooby and Shaggy
tell the gang
about the monster.

They look for

the monster.

They do not see it.

Scooby and Shaggy spot

something else—

the hot dog stand!
They forget about
the monster.

The friends find
their seats.
The race starts!

The cars drive very fast!
Scooby and Shaggy lean
over the railing.

One car makes a cloud
of smoke.
Scooby and Shaggy
get scared.

Scooby and Shaggy jump
onto the track.
They see the monster again!

Ahh!

Scooby and Shaggy jump

off the track.

They tell Fred, Velma,
and Daphne that they saw
the monster again.

Scooby and Shaggy

want to leave.

The others want to stay.

Velma says Shaggy and Scooby

can have Scooby Snacks!

The snacks are in the

Mystery Machine.

Velma looks for the snacks.

She can't find them.

Now everyone gets in the
Mystery Machine to look.
Scooby and Shaggy find
the Scooby Snacks!

Zoinks!

The monster is back!

Fred drives away.

The monster chases them.

More monsters join
the chase!

Fred drives onto
the racetrack.
The crowd cheers!

Velma thinks that
is strange.

She has an idea.
She grabs the tickets
from the racetrack.
She reads that the
monsters chasing them
are monster *trucks*!

The gang crosses
the finish line first.

The gang has won
the monster truck race!

SNACK SNATCHER

by Gail Herman

illustrated by Duendes del Sur

Random House 🏠 New York

Scooby and Shaggy

enter a baking contest.

The winner gets free pizza for a whole year!

Fred, Velma, and Daphne
gather the supplies.

Scooby and Shaggy

get a pizza.

They are hungry!

Scooby and Shaggy put on
aprons and chef hats.

Shaggy and Scooby
are sleepy!
They need to finish baking.
Then they can nap.

Scooby and Shaggy
work quickly.
They stir and roll and chop.

Scooby and Shaggy put
the food in the oven.
They fall asleep!

Daphne, Fred, and Velma
hear a woman scream.
The woman drops her
baking supplies.

She says there is a
monster by her table!

They all hear
a rumbling noise.

Daphne, Fred, and Velma
rush over.
They see a big blob.

It is Scooby and Shaggy!
The gang wakes them
from their nap.

The gang tells Scooby
and Shaggy
about the monster.
Bing!
The oven timer goes off.

Scooby and Shaggy

run to the oven.

Shaggy opens it.
It is empty.
The monster took
their food!

The gang sees handprints
on the oven.
They see paw prints
on the floor.

Scooby and Shaggy
are scared!
Velma gives them
Scooby Snacks.

Fred, Daphne, and Velma
follow the paw prints.

Scooby and Shaggy find
a trail of crumbs.

The crumbs lead to where Scooby and Shaggy were napping.

Velma, Fred, and Daphne
are there, too.
Scooby bumps into Velma!

Velma sees crumbs
on Scooby's paw.
Scooby says he ate some
of the snack they baked.

Fred sees crumbs
on Shaggy's shirt.
Shaggy says he ate some
of the snack they baked, too.

There is no monster!
The woman thought
Scooby and Shaggy were
a monster when they
were asleep!

They left the handprints
and paw prints.
The mystery is solved!

Scooby and Shaggy
are out of the contest.
Now they can eat
everyone else's food!